Aunt Rosa's House

By Maggie Moran

Illustrations by Chie Sasaki

New Voices Publishing
Wilmington, Massachusetts

Text Copyright © 2002 Margaret A. Moran
Illustrations Copyright © 2002 KidsTerrain, Inc.

For information regarding permission, please write to:
Permissions Department, New Voices Publishing,
P.O. Box 560, Wilmington, Massachusetts, 01887.

Book Design, Typography & Composition by: Arrow Graphics, Inc.
Printed in China

Published by:
New Voices Publishing,
a division of KidsTerrain, Inc.
P.O. Box 560
Wilmington, MA 01887

**Publisher's Cataloging-in-Publication
(Provided by Quality Books, Inc.)**

Moran, Maggie A.
     Aunt Rosa's house / by Maggie Moran ; illustrations
by Chie Sasaki.—1st ed.
     p. cm.
     SUMMARY: Miguel's Aunt Rosa is special, and Miguel
loves to visit her. She's always interested in him, and
she always teaches him things—like how to play chess
and what his special Spanish heritage means.
     Audience: Ages 4-8
     LCCN 2001096461
     ISBN: 1-931642-04-4

     1. Aunts—Juvenile fiction. 2. Spanish Americans—
Juvenile fiction. [1. Aunts—Fiction. 2. Spanish
Americans—Fiction.]   I. Sasaki, Chie. II. Title

PZ7.M78825Au 2002   [E]
                         QBI33-161

First Edition: June 2002
10 9 8 7 6 5 4 3 2 1

Dedication

For Ellen and Shayne

My deepest gratitude goes to Rita Schiano for her tireless
editing and artistic direction. Her wisdom and attention
to thoughtful detail bring this story to life. Without her
persistence and dedication, this book would not have
been published. Thank you for making this happen.
To Chie Sasaki for her artistic attention
and dedication to critical detail.
And for all who believe in the importance of
"Listening and Talking to Kids," I thank you
from the bottom of my heart.

Miguel was very excited when he awoke this morning. He was going to spend the day at Aunt Rosa's house.

Aunt Rosa was his mother's aunt. She moved here from Spain several years ago and Miguel loved to listen to her stories about *España*.

Miguel's mother and father had to go away for the day and Aunt Rosa was going to take care of him. He was always happy to visit with his Aunt Rosa and to spend time with her at her house.

"Miguel," his mother called to him. "Are you ready to go?"

"I'm ready," he called back to her.

Aunt Rosa lived in a yellow house with green
shutters and a big front porch with two rocking
chairs. Miguel loved to sit with his aunt and rock
and talk and eat chocolate chip cookies.

Sometimes when Miguel visited Aunt Rosa, he would
help her pick beautiful, colorful flowers from her
garden to put in the big flowerpot she kept next to
the front door of the porch. Miguel liked doing that.

But most of all, Miguel loved Aunt Rosa because
she was easy to talk with. Aunt Rosa always listened
to him and that made Miguel feel special.

When Miguel and his parents arrived at Aunt Rosa's, Miguel jumped out of the car and ran up the porch stairs to the front door. He rang the doorbell and waited rather impatiently.

The front door, painted red to complement the shutters, opened and there stood Aunt Rosa with a big smile on her face.

"*Miguelito*!" she hugged him, rocking back and forth. "You look so *muy guapo* today."

Miguel gave his aunt a warm smile. He loved the way she talked; how she mixed Spanish words together with English ones. Miguel learned many Spanish words and phrases from his Aunt Rosa.

Miguel waved goodbye to his parents.

"So, *Miguelito*, what would you like to do today?"

He answered, "Play with the computer!"

"*Si*. Let's go downstairs," Aunt Rosa said.

Miguel and Aunt Rosa went down the stairs and sat together at the computer.

Miguel loved the computer and he loved playing chess on Aunt Rosa's computer. Miguel knew that he could not play with the computer unless Aunt Rosa was with him.

"So, do you want to play chess?" Aunt Rosa asked.

"*Sí, tía Rosa,*" answered Miguel.

"Do you remember how to use the computer?" asked Aunt Rosa.

"I think so," said Miguel.

"Show me what you remember and we'll go from there."

Miguel pushed a button, and then placed the chess game CD into the computer.

Aunt Rosa reminded Miguel what he could do with the computer and what he could not do. Since Aunt Rosa used her computer for work, Miguel knew that he couldn't press certain buttons. He had to be very careful with the computer, or he might lose some of Aunt Rosa's important information.

Miguel and Aunt Rosa played chess together. She taught him about *estrategia*. They laughed and talked and had lots of fun.

After awhile, Aunt Rosa looked at her watch. "Ah!" she said. "We almost forgot lunch. Are you hungry?"

Miguel was busy playing his game so he shook his head, "yes."

"How about going upstairs now and we'll have hot dogs?" she said.

Miguel turned off the game, just the way Aunt Rosa taught him to do.

They went upstairs and Aunt Rosa began to boil hot dogs in the pan, just the way Miguel liked them.

Miguel gathered plates from the cabinet and mustard and ketchup from the refrigerator while Aunt Rosa filled a basket with hot dog rolls.

Aunt Rosa placed the hot dogs in the rolls and gave one to Miguel. Miguel poured ketchup and mustard all over his hot dog.

During lunch, Miguel told Aunt Rosa about school, his teacher, and about his friends Maria and David. Miguel liked school a lot and he liked playing with his friends. He told Aunt Rosa that he and his friends played games and rode their bikes and talked a lot, too.

He also told her that sometimes things happen that make him sad.

"When does that happen?" asked Aunt Rosa.

"Well, it's like when other kids don't want to play with me and when they don't want to listen to me," said Miguel.

"And why is that?" asked Aunt Rosa.

"I don't know. Maybe because I want to show them how to play chess and they don't want to play chess."

Miguel also told Aunt Rosa about another friend who had made new friends and didn't want to play with him anymore.

"Well, it sounds like Maria and David like the same things you do, *si*? And those other boys and girls just like different things," Aunt Rosa said. "And that's—how you say?—okay."

Aunt Rosa asked Miguel if there were boys and girls that he didn't like to play with, and Miguel said, "*Si*."

"Ah, Miguel, even you feel that way sometimes. You don't have to be friends with everyone," said Aunt Rosa. "But it is important to be nice to everyone."

Miguel shook his head, indicating that he understood.

"Would you like to talk about it some more?"

"Maybe later," answered Miguel.

Miguel finished his hot dog and eyed the big cookie jar on the counter next to the refrigerator. Aunt Rosa always kept it full of all different kinds of cookies. Especially Miguel's favorite: chocolate chip.

"Can I go outside and play in the backyard?" Miguel asked.

"Go ahead, Miguel," Aunt Rosa said. "I'll be out in a few minutes."

Miguel grabbed his soccer ball and lingered by the cookie jar as he headed to the back door.

Aunt Rosa laughed heartily. Miguel loved his aunt's laugh. It made him smile.

"Take some cookies with you," she said, still laughing.

Aunt Rosa had a giant maple tree in the middle of her backyard. Miguel lay on his back and looked up at the tree and imagined it was the olive tree from Aunt Rosa's house in Spain. Some of his friends had apple trees, pear trees, and even cherry trees. But no one had an olive tree like his Aunt Rosa had in Spain.

"It's a beautiful tree, isn't it, Miguel?" Aunt Rosa said.

Miguel nodded. "But don't you miss your olive tree, Aunt Rosa?"

"Sometimes. But this tree is so beautiful and different. Did I tell you it's over 100 years old?"

Miguel sat up. "That's pretty old, Aunt Rosa. Is the tree going to die soon?"

"Oh, no, *Miguelito*. That tree will be around for a long, long time."

"Just like you," Miguel said.

"*Sí*, Miguel. I certainly hope so!" answered Aunt Rosa.

"Me, too!" said Miguel.

Aunt Rosa watched with joy as Miguel ran up and down the yard kicking his soccer ball, bouncing it off his head, and raising his arms in victory when he scored an imaginary goal.

All of a sudden, Miguel ran up to Aunt Rosa and said, "Can we look at the pictures of your house in Spain?"

"*Sí*, why don't you come in the house and we'll have some juice, too," said Aunt Rosa.

They went inside, got some juice and the photo album, and settled on the big sofa in Aunt Rosa's living room.

Together they looked through the photo album bursting
with pictures. Miguel especially liked the picture of
Aunt Rosa's *casa* in Spain, the one with the olive tree
in the backyard. Aunt Rosa told him stories about her
life in *mi tierra natal*. Stories about the Alhambra
—the grand royal palace in Granada, the city where
their family lived for many generations.

While they were looking through the pictures, Miguel asked Aunt Rosa if he could have a sleepover sometime. He wanted to spend more time with Aunt Rosa, more than just a day. He was happy here.

"And maybe we can stay up all night and you can tell me about Spain. And maybe I can tell you things about me, too."

Aunt Rosa gave Miguel a big smile and said, "*Fantástico, Miguelito*! We'll ask your mother and father if it is okay with them."

Later that afternoon when Miguel's mother and father arrived to take him home, he said, "Can I have a sleepover the next time I come?"

"If it's all right with Aunt Rosa, then it's fine with us," said his mother.

"*Bravo!*" yelled Miguel.

Aunt Rosa looked at him and gave him a wink.
"See you at the sleepover."

Miguel gave her a big hug.

"Te quiero, tía Rosa, y me gusta tu casa!"

Questions:

Do you know anyone like Aunt Rosa?
Do you visit her like Miguel does?
Who makes you feel good?
What makes you feel good/happy?
Who makes you feel sad?
What makes you feel sad?
What do you know about your family's heritage?